The Gnomes of Fibberton

Written by **Becky Bell**
Illustrated by **Aadil Khan**

Don't get carried away!
Scan the QR code in the middle
of the book to sing along!

Becky Bell

Printed in China

Copyright © 2024,
The Incomprehensibly Unimaginable Consortium Incorporated.
All rights reserved.

No part of this publication may be reproduced,
distributed, or transmitted in any form or by any means,
including photocopying, recording,
or other electronic or mechanical methods,
without the prior written permission of the publisher,
except in the case of brief quotations embodied
in critical reviews and certain other noncommercial
uses permitted by copyright law.

I dedicate this book to my Lord.
Only through his graciousness
is this work possible.

...in a place both far away, and yet far too close...

...deep underground is a land known as Fibberton.

Grouchy little creatures are busy scrawling in their dusty tomes, a special number, a secret number...

...next to the name and picture of each newborn child.

These unhappy little creatures are known only to a few, and now they are known to you, as the Gnomes of Fibberton.

Fibberton isn't known as a place for having fun.
In Fibberton, it is always either too hot...

...or too cold

The air smells like sweaty feet, there is never a comfortable seat to be found, and all of the toys have been broken long, long ago.

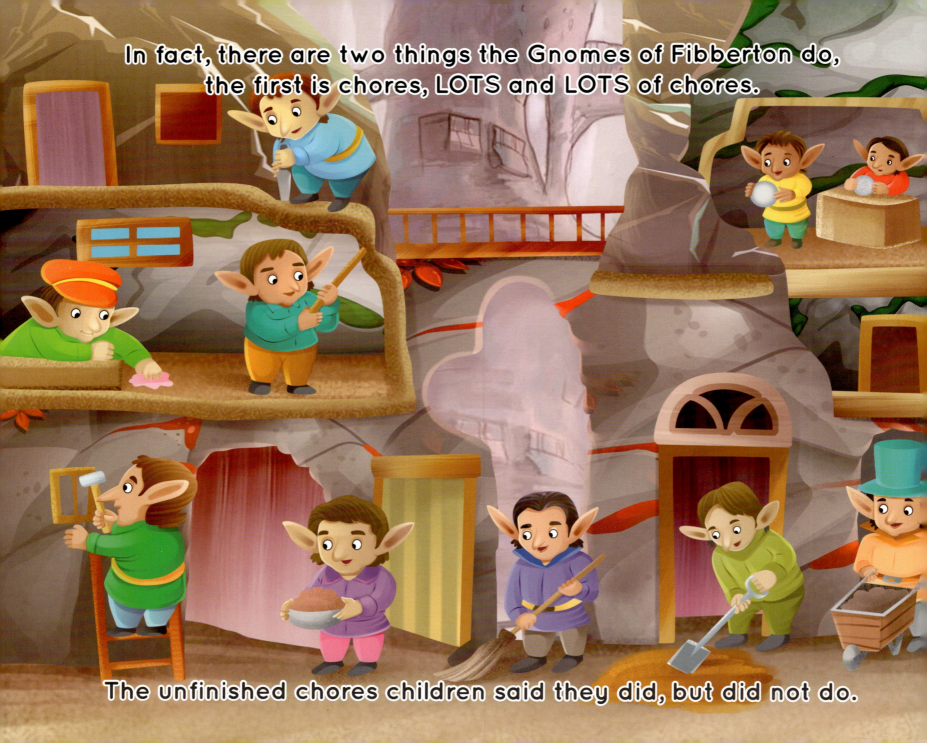

In fact, there are two things the Gnomes of Fibberton do, the first is chores, LOTS and LOTS of chores.

The unfinished chores children said they did, but did not do.

Which leads us to the second thing that the Gnomes of Fibberton do...

One has been found in a pair of smelly old shoes...

...another inside a tub of ice cream in the freezer...

...they have even been known to hide in cookie jars!

If you happen to spot them, they turn into statues that parents ignore...

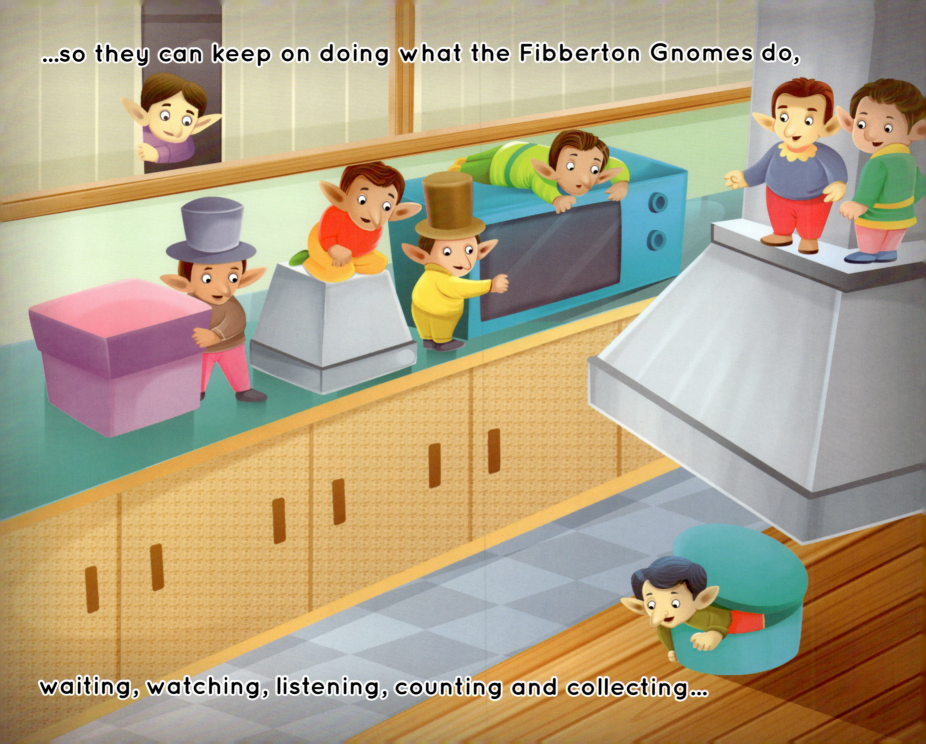

...FIBS! You see, when a child doesn't tell the truth, they create a fib. To you and me a fib is just a sound spoken and then gone.

To the Gnomes of Fibberton, fibs are tiny, awful treasures...

...which they go about greedily collecting,

adding them up, one by one...

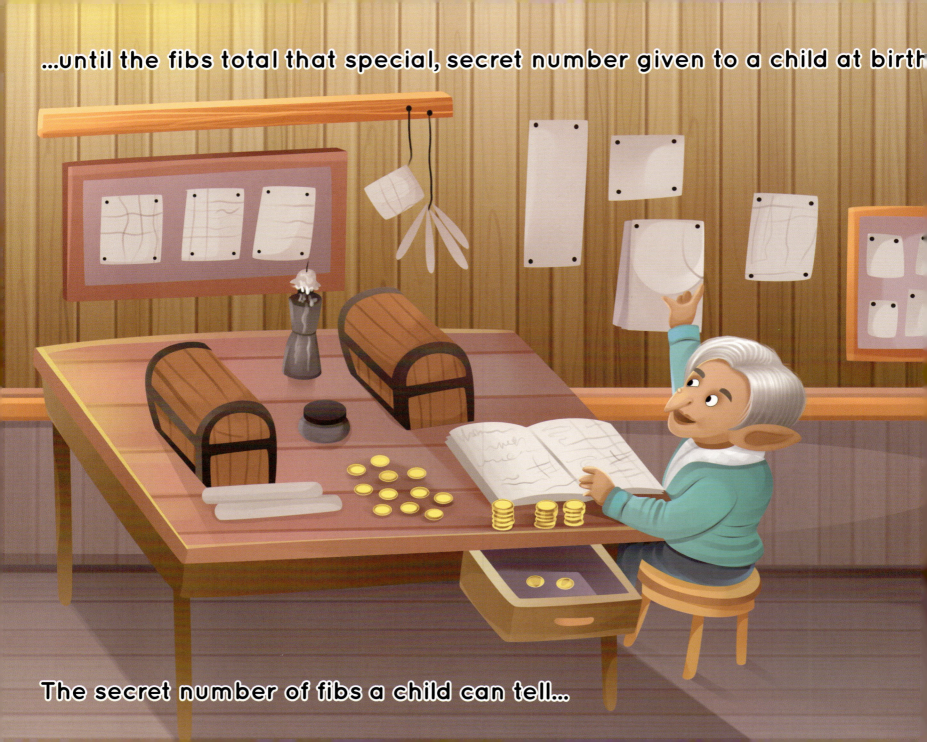

...until the fibs total that special, secret number given to a child at birth.

The secret number of fibs a child can tell...

...before the Gnomes of Fibberton come...

...when you feed your vegetables to the dog,

or don't clean up your room,

just remember to tell the truth,